Oliver Who Would Not Sleep!

To the memory of Seymour Regent and
Sharon Clair, and for all my insomniac friends—M. B.

For John and Avis—N. M.

Text copyright © 2007 by Mara Bergman
Illustrations copyright © 2007 by Nick Maland

Library of Congress Cataloging-in-Publication Data

Bergman, Mara.
Oliver who would not sleep! / Mara Bergman ; Nick Maland. — 1st ed.   p. cm.
Summary: Oliver Donnington Rimington-Sneep avoids falling asleep by flying his rocket ship to Mars.
ISBN-13: 978-0-439-92826-7   ISBN-10: 0-439-92826-5
[1. Bedtime—Fiction. 2. Rockets (Aeronautics)—Fiction. 3. Space flight to Mars—Fiction. 4. Stories in rhyme.]
I. Maland, Nick, ill. II. Title. PZ8.3.B39653Oli 2007 [E]—dc22 2006030775

The text type was set in 21-pt. Charlotte Book. The display type was set in Chub.
Design by Lillie Mear

10 9 8 7 6 5 4 3 2 1   07 08 09 10 11
Printed in China
First edition, September 2007

Oliver
Who Would Not
Sleep!

MARA BERGMAN ✳ NICK MALAND

ARTHUR A. LEVINE BOOKS
AN IMPRINT OF SCHOLASTIC INC.

Oliver Donnington Rimington-Sneep

COULDN'T and DIDN'T

and WOULD NOT SLEEP!

It wasn't that he
was afraid of the dark,
of monsters or robbers
or sounds from the park,

but that...

Oliver Donnington Rimington-Sneep
liked staying awake
more than going to sleep.

After his parents had kissed him good night,

they tucked him in snugly and turned off the light.

Straightaway Oliver bounced out of bed.

He painted...

and drew...

did magic...

and read.

He raced all his cars,

then he raced them some more,

and just as he blasted his rocket he saw...

with rooftops and trees and an owl in flight.

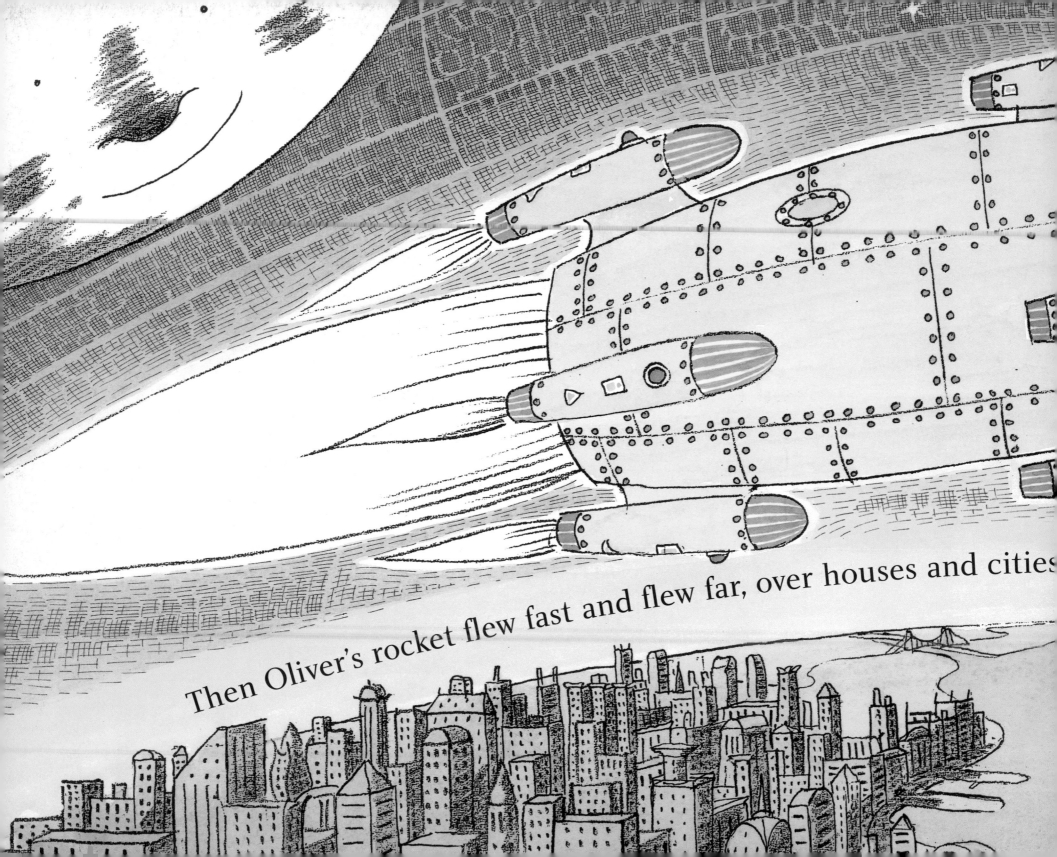

Then Oliver's rocket flew fast and flew far, over houses and cities

nd up to the stars, past the moon and past comets till...

it landed on Mars –
a wonderful, fabulous,
wide-open place
smack-dab in the middle
of all that dark space.

Oliver stood and Oliver
stared, without even being
the slightest bit scared.

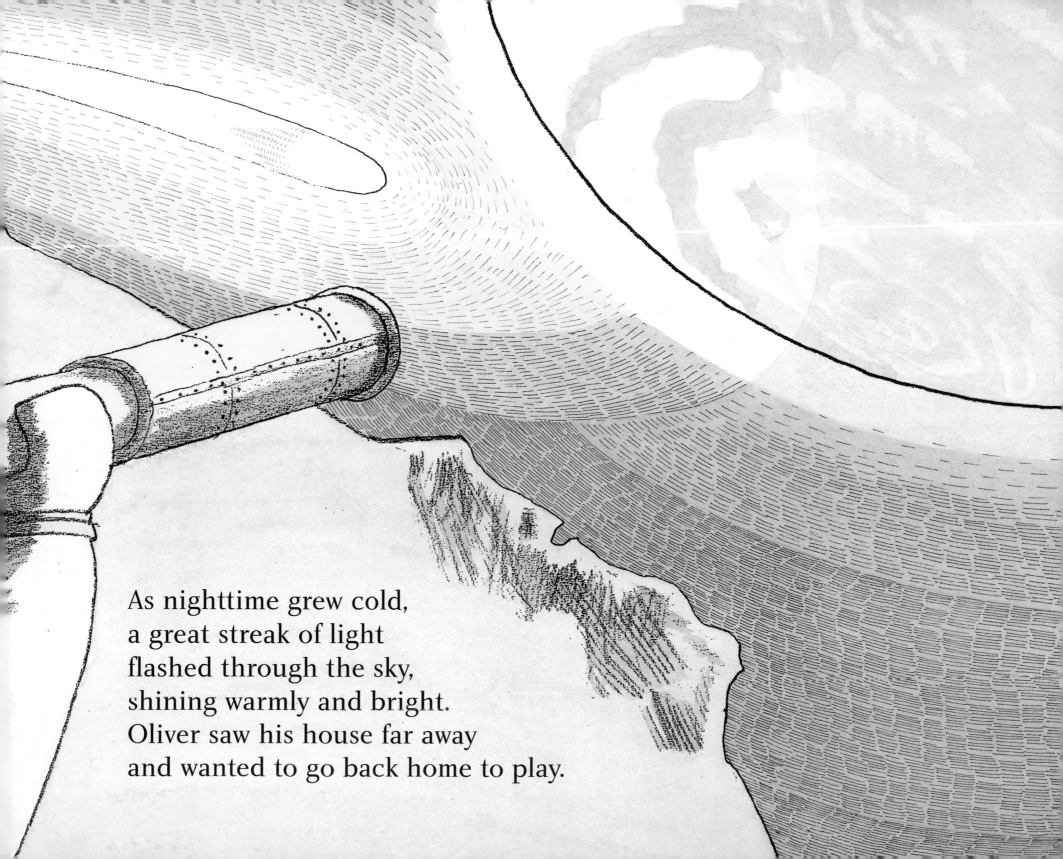

As nighttime grew cold,
a great streak of light
flashed through the sky,
shining warmly and bright.
Oliver saw his house far away
and wanted to go back home to play.

Through outer space,

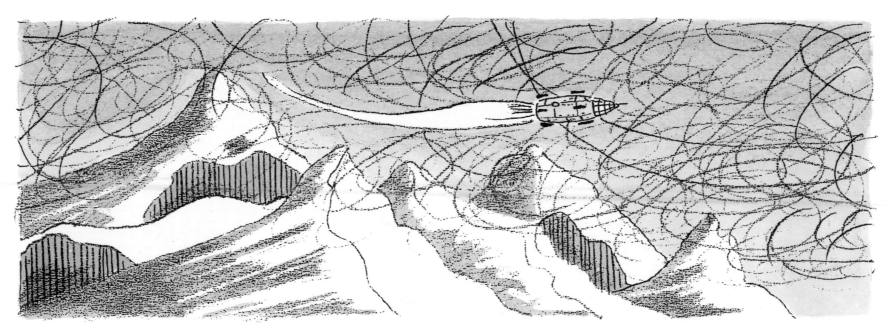

over mountains and seas,

through clouds, over rooftops

and branches of trees…

the rocket soared back to Oliver's room,
where all of his cuddlies looked cozy and warm.

Bat and Owl, Fox and Ted
were waiting for him to climb into bed.

So with a great big stretch

and a great long *yawn...*

Oliver Donnington Rimington-Sneep

finally... finally...

finally... finally...

finally... *finally...*

fell fast asleep.

DATE DUE